Cane Boy

Written By:

Chiara Agro (12 years old)

Amadeo Agro (9 years old)

Peter Tassi (old)

Edited By:

Sharon Boase

Illustrations by:

Lizy J Campbell

A proud supporter of Tunnel to Towers Foundation.

Fifty percent of all net revenues paid to authors are

donated to t2t.

I walk through the alley to get to school because it's the fastest way.

If I took the other way, it would take way too long to get to school.

I don't like getting up too early. When I do, I'm tired all day. I prefer to go to bed late and sleep in a bit.

My Mom always tells me I should get to sleep earlier.

What time do you think school should start in the morning?

Are you tired while you are in school?

Should school have a rest or sleep time?

I don't like taking the alley because Devlin, Donny and Baden are always waiting for me.

They wait for other kids as well.

They are bullies and can be very mean. I have to give them my lunch money to get past them. Sometimes they just like pushing people around.

Have you ever been bullied?

Why do some kids become bullies?

Have you ever seen someone bullied and wondered what to do?

Mom made my lunch so she didn't give me any money.

Because I didn't have money, Devlin, Donny and Baden started pushing me around until I fell to the ground.

Devlin then reached down and took my favorite hat.

Donny said,

"No lunch money, Ben? That's too bad. We'll just take your hat."

Do you bring a lunch from home or do you get lunch at school?

What is your favourite lunch?

Does eating lunch help you do better in school?

When I fell, I turned and saw an old man at the end of the alley. He was sitting on a wooden box carving a long piece of wood.

He looked peaceful and kind.

I was embarrassed because he saw everything that had happened.

Have you ever seen someone on the streets making something beautiful?

Can someone make money selling their work on the street?

What kinds of things would you like to see people make on the streets?

I felt ashamed as I approached him. He called out to me,

"Hey, young fellow, come here."

I was afraid.

I approached him and saw he was carving a beautiful cane. There were many nice-looking canes behind him, leaning against the fence.

The one he was just finishing was the most beautiful of all.

Can you remember meeting someone new and interesting?

Who is the most fun person you ever met?

Who would you like to meet?

He handed me the cane and said, "Here, this is for you."

It had the moon carved towards the bottom end and a sun carved near the top. I fell in love with it.

I said to him,

"I can't take this, I have no money to pay you."

He replied: "It's a gift. Never let it leave your side. Use it to do good and never give it away."

I asked him his name. He answered, "Augustine."

What is the best gift someone could give you?

What superpower would you like to have?

Do you know someone who makes the world a better place?

As I began to leave, he said:

"Now Remember young fellow, never give up on your dreams. And never let that cane leave your side."

I answered,

"I won't Mr. Augustine."

I began to leave, admiring my beautiful, new cane. I walked a few feet and then turned back to thank him again but he was gone.

It was as if he had disappeared.

What do you think happened to Mr. Augustine?

Why is it so important to say "thank you?"

What you want to be when you grow up?

I continued on my way to school, stopping at a street corner. A mother and her little girl stood beside me.

We waited for our crossing guard, Mr. Bigfoot, to hold up his sign so we could cross. He was always concerned about our safety. He wanted us to be safe and happy.

We called him Mr. Bigfoot because he had very big feet.

Do the kids at your school always obey the crossing guard?

What street safety rules should you always follow?

Do you know anyone who is as nice and caring as Mr. Bigfoot?

Suddenly, the little girl left her mother's side and ran out onto the street.

A car was approaching, going very fast.

Her mother yelled, "Stella, stop!"

With my cane in hand, I stretched out my arm and yelled, "Stop!" I felt a jolt of electricity coming from the cane.

The car stopped immediately. Everyone was surprised.

I asked myself: "Was it my booming voice? Was it my cane?
Was it someone reaching down from above?"

What do you think caused the car to stop?

Do you always look both ways before crossing the street?

Are there lights and signs that tell you when it is safe to cross on your street?

Stella's mom ran out onto the road, picked up Stella and carried her to safety. The car sped off.

Stella's mom cried out,

"It's a miracle, it's a miracle!"

I continued on to school. All the way I was thinking about what had just

happened and how happy I was.

Then I remembered Math class.

What is your favourite subject? Why?

What subject do you dislike the most? Why?

What things have happened in your life that you just can't explain?

I wasn't happy to be in Math class. I never did well in Math.

Today was my turn to go to the board and answer the questions.

I eventually heard those dreaded words from my Math teacher, Miss Festernots,
"Ben, your turn to go to the board and answer the questions."

I was as afraid of the Math questions as I was of Miss Festernots. She was strict and expected us to know our Math.

Do you get nervous when you have to stand up in front of people?

How do teachers show they care for you?

What are you most afraid of?

The last time I was at the board, I answered almost every question wrong.

Miss Festernots was not happy.

Lezabel, who sits next to me, said I was stupid. I used to like her because she has pretty hair and a nice smile.

After she called me stupid, I didn't like her as much. I really wanted to answer the questions right this time to show Lezabel that I'm not stupid.

I also wanted Miss Festernots to be happy.

Do you believe everyone has a talent?

What is your special talent?

Should you forgive someone who calls you a name?

I walked to the board and Miss Festernots asked me,

"Ben, what are you doing with that cane?"

I told her that it was a gift and that it brought me luck. I asked her if I could keep it with me. I was happy when she nodded, *yes*.

Why do you think Mr. Augustine gave Ben the cane?

Do you have something special that you like to keep with you?

Where do you get your strength from?

As I wrote the answers on the board, I could feel little zaps of electricity coming from my cane. I answered every question perfectly.

It may have been because of the extra hours I studied with the Math tutor my father got me. Or maybe it was my new cane.

After writing the answer to the last question, Miss Festernots yelled,

"Perfect score, Ben!"

The class clapped for me, even Lezabel.

Do you think it was the cane or the extra studying that made Ben so smart?

Would you like a group of people to clap when you do something special?

Do you have a favourite friend?

I had to put my cane to the test.

I decided I would not tell Mom and Dad about my cane or my day.

On my way home I held my cane tight and asked that my Mom would make my favourite desert: a red velvet cake.

When you are confused, what do you do to find an answer?

If Ben's cane is magical, what other powers can it give him?

We would like to hear from you at supercaneboy@yahoo.com

ADD YOUR COLOUR TO THE STORY

The End!

Look out for more Cane Boy books
coming soon!

Written By:

Chiara Agro (12 years old)

Amadeo Agro (9 years old)

Peter Tassi (old)

Edited by:

Sharon Boase

Illustrations by:

Lizy J Campbell

Manufactured by Amazon.ca
Bolton, ON